GRAY RABBIT'S
FAVORITE THINGS

ALAN BAKER

KINGFISHER
NEW YORK

KINGFISHER
LONDON & NEW YORK

First published 1994 by Kingfisher
This edition published 2017 by Kingfisher
Published in the United States by Kingfisher,
175 Fifth Ave., New York, NY 10010
Kingfisher is an imprint of Macmillan Children's Books, London.
All rights reserved.

Copyright © Alan Baker 1994

Distributed in the U.S. and Canada by Macmillan,
175 Fifth Ave., New York, NY 10010

Library of Congress Cataloging-in-Publication data
has been applied for.

ISBN: 978-0-7534-7338-2 (HB)
ISBN: 978-0-7534-7357-3 (PB)

Kingfisher books are available for special promotions
and premiums. For details contact: Special Markets
Department, Macmillan, 175 Fifth Ave.,
New York, NY 10010.

For more information, please visit
www.kingfisherbooks.com

Printed in China
9 8 7 6 5 4 3 2 1
1TR/1216/WKT/UG/157MA

One morning Gray Rabbit could
not find his favorite book.

It's time to clean up, thought Rabbit.
First let's sort out the wooden animals.

There were two of each kind—just like in Noah's ark.

But one thing was not an animal.
What was the odd one out?

A teaspoon.

So Rabbit sorted out his cups and saucers.
But one thing did not belong.
What was it?

A paintbrush.

Rabbit gathered up his paints and brushes and made a useful sign. Now what was the odd one out?

A red and yellow polka-dot ball.

Rabbit found all his round things.
Hey, stop rolling away!
But one thing did not belong.
What was it?

A purple vase.
Where can that go? thought Rabbit.
It's the only vase I have.

Then he matched it up with all the other purple things. But something wasn't purple. What was it?

A duck. That belonged with the other stuffed animals, so Rabbit lined them all up in a row.

Now what did not belong?

A block.

There were lots and lots of blocks.
How could Rabbit sort them out?

First he built a square
of red blocks,

then a wall
of green blocks.

The yellow blocks made a tower.
What was that among the blue blocks?

Look! Rabbit's favorite book.
I'll sort out the blue blocks,
he thought, then I'll read
my story.

At last!